Ming

Abbasids

Mughals

Aceh

N
W E
S

First published in the United Kingdom
in 1445 AH (2024 CE) by
Learning Roots Ltd.
London, United Kingdom
www.learningroots.com

Copyright © Learning Roots, 2024
Authored by Dr. Azhar Majothi and Zaheer Khatri
Project managed by Yasmin Mussa
Layout and Illustrations by Fatima Zahur, Deni Nugroho,
Pagudar Borneo, Mariana Gutiez and Jannah Haque

Notice of Rights

Acknowledgments
The publisher thanks Allāh, Lord of the worlds, for making this publication possible.

British Library Cataloguing in Publication Data
A CIP catalogue record for this book is available from the British Library.

Printed and bound in China
ISBN: 978-1-915381-02-6

LEARNING ROOTS

The Amazing Muslim Worlds

Discover over 1400 years of epic Islamic history

Contents

· · · · · · · · · · · · · · · ·

You're part of a great Ummah

The **Amazing Muslim Worlds** walks children through a selection of 12 empires, sultanates and Muslim civilisations throughout history, demonstrating the beautiful, rich diversity of our Ummah. Children from all walks of life will find a Muslim World they can relate to and discover an array of other inspiring cultures, all strengthened by the common thread of faith.

This book is designed as a child's first step in discovering Islamic history, emphasising the hugely positive contributions of Muslims through the ages. It aims to instil a sense of identity, belonging and inspiration.

Most importantly, each section concludes with how the religion of Islam has been the core source behind the greatness that these empires achieved. Each dynasty demonstrates qualities that are deeply rooted in Islam's spiritual core. This book also invites children to reflect on their aspirations for a positive, faith-inspired contribution.

In the discourse of Islamic history, there tends to be a heavy focus on worldly achievements such as the building of magnificent structures, the invention of new technologies, the accumulation of wealth and the conquering of new territories. However, the Muslim lens is incomplete without the hereafter.

The extraordinary achievements of many key Muslim figures had motivations beyond this world. The hereafter is where Muslims anticipate a remarkable reward for their excellent work in this world. This book helps children to grasp a holistic understanding of an outstanding legacy that encompasses both this world and the next.

Andalucia

Ottomans

Seljuks

Ayyubia

Umayyids

Abbasids

Mali

Mamluks

Rashidun

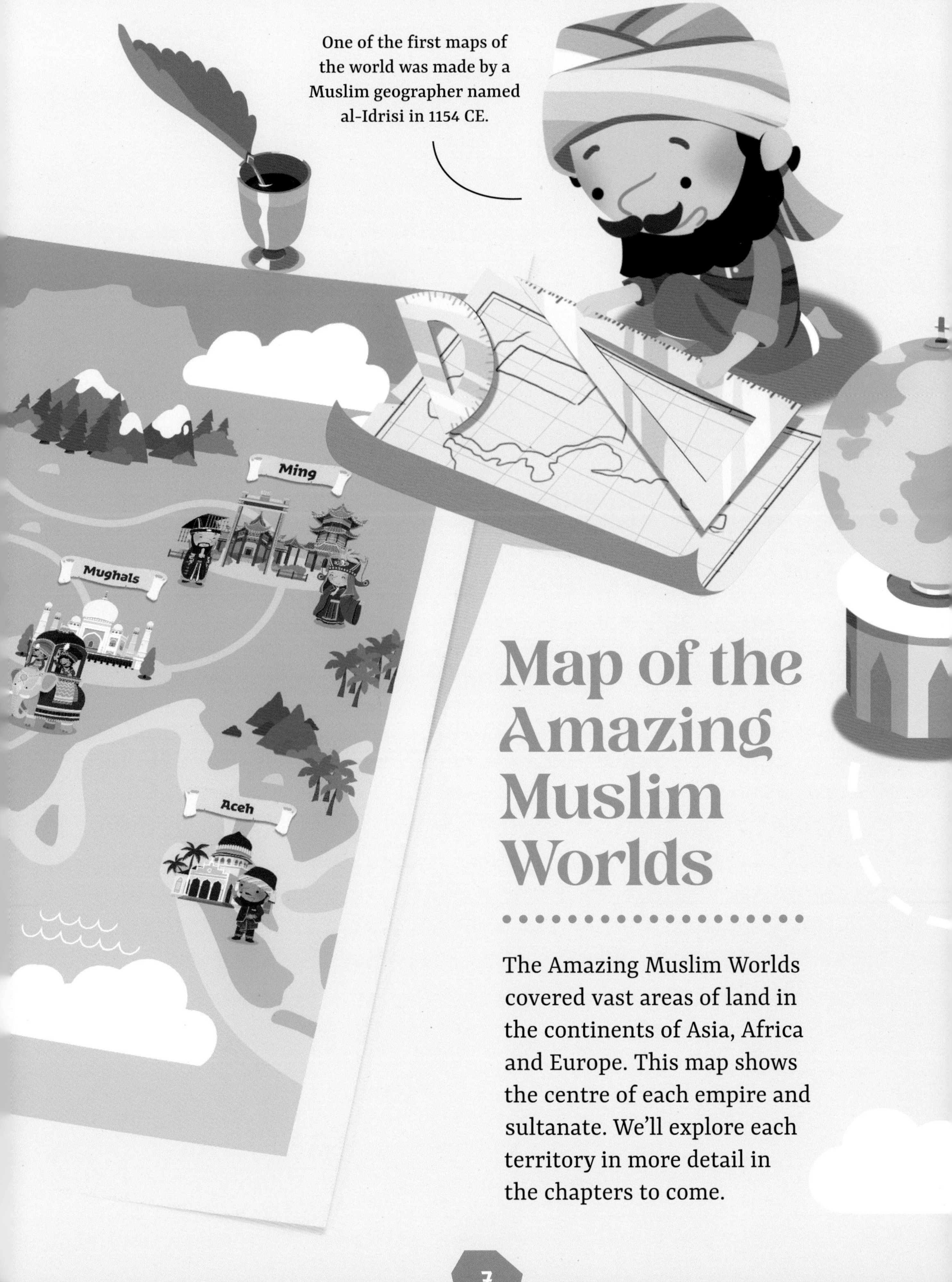

One of the first maps of the world was made by a Muslim geographer named al-Idrisi in 1154 CE.

Ming

Mughals

Aceh

Map of the Amazing Muslim Worlds

The Amazing Muslim Worlds covered vast areas of land in the continents of Asia, Africa and Europe. This map shows the centre of each empire and sultanate. We'll explore each territory in more detail in the chapters to come.

Timeline of the Amazing Muslim Worlds

The Amazing Muslim Worlds used the Hijri calendar (AH), which starts from when the Prophet Muhammad ﷺ migrated from Makkah to Madinah. When we discover each 'World' in detail, we'll mention the dates again using the Gregorian calendar (CE).

3
Awesome Andalusians
92–897 AH
(805 years)

4
Astounding Abbasids
133–923 AH
(790 years)

2
Ambitious Umayyads
41–133 AH
(92 years)

1
Righteous Rashiduns
11–41 AH
(30 years)

5

Sensational Seljuks

429–590 AH
(161 years)

6

Admirable Ayyubids

567–742 AH
(175 years)

7

Magnificent Mali

628–1083 AH
(455 years)

8

Marvelous Mamluks

648–923 AH
(275 years)

9

Outstanding Ottomans

699–1341 AH
(642 years)

10

Charming Chinese Muslims

770–1054 AH
(284 years)

11

Amazing Aceh

902–1321 AH
(419 years)

12

Mighty Mughals

933–1274 AH
(341 years)

The Righteous Rashiduns

Lasted for 30 years from 632 to 661 CE

A fter the death of Prophet Muhammad ﷺ, his four closest Companions, Abu Bakr, Umar, Uthman and Ali continued to rule over the first Muslim empire. They were called the 'Rightly-Guided Caliphs'. In just 30 years, they spread the message of Islam in Africa and Asia and defeated the both the mighty Roman and Persian Empires.

At the time of the Prophet ﷺ, all of Arabia had accepted Islam. But when he passed away, many tribes rebelled, leaving the blessed cities of Madinah and Makkah as the only places that held on to Islam. Thanks to some brave decisions by the first Caliph Abu Bakr, the Muslims defeated the rebels and united Arabia again under the banner of Islam.

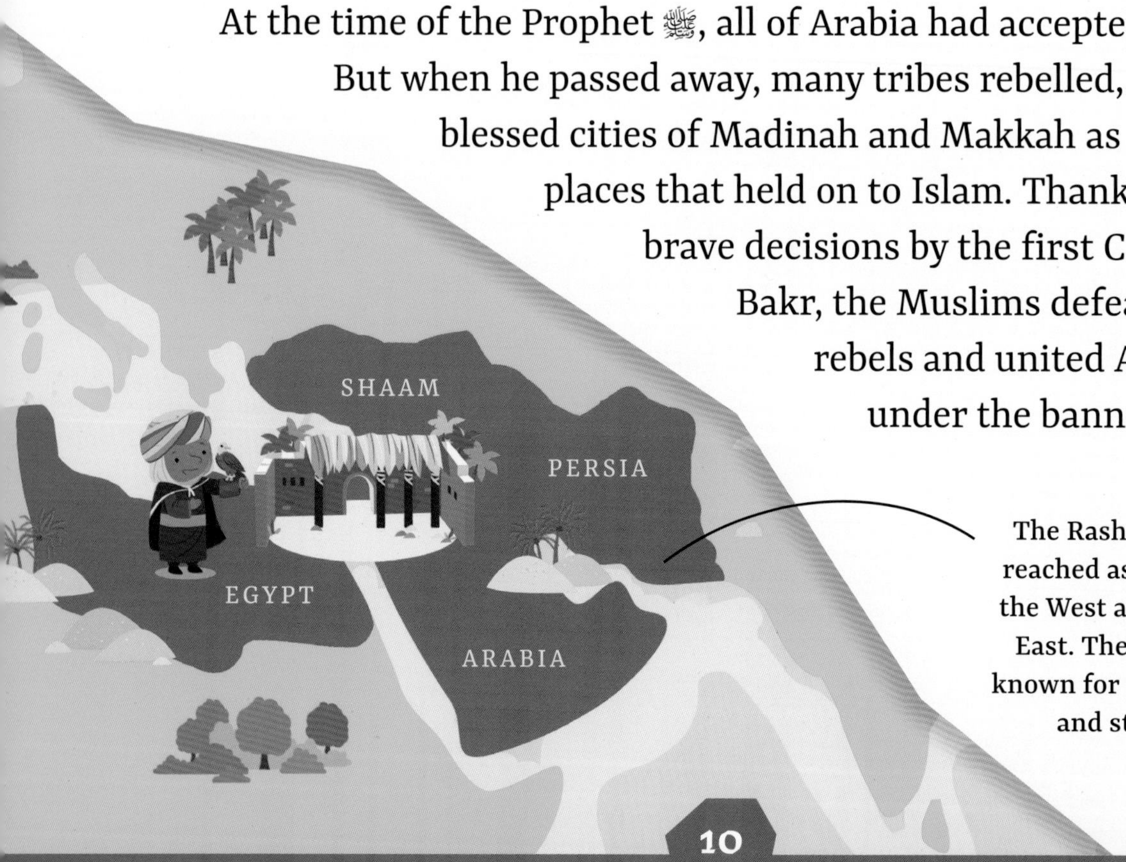

SHAAM

PERSIA

EGYPT

ARABIA

The Rashidun Caliphate reached as far as Egypt in the West and Persia in the East. The Caliphate was known for its justice, peace and strong faith.

Changing the World

Before the Prophet ﷺ passed away, he told his Companions to follow the way of the Rightly-Guided Caliphs. And so, the early Muslims were very loyal to their leaders. This unity helped turn the humble capital of Madinah into a global superpower.

The two biggest rivals at the time were the giant Roman Empire to the West and the great Persian Empire to the East. Despite their well-trained troops and better weapons, they were no match for the Muslims who overcame them with clever battle plans, faith and strong hearts.

The Companions also took on the all-important task of teaching

Abu Bakr
(d. 634 CE)

Abu Bakr was the first ruler of the Rashidun Caliphate. He was the Prophet's ﷺ best friend and ruled for two years. Despite opposition, he made key decisions that protected Islam, spread the message and secured a bright future for its followers.

their children and new Muslims about the wonders of the Quran. Meanwhile, Companions like Aisha, the mother of the believers, and Abu Hurayrah also taught people the hadith of the Prophet ﷺ so that the message of Islam would live long after them.

Umar bin al-Khattab
(d. 644 CE)

Umar was one of the strongest men in Makkah, and when he became Muslim, no one dared insult Islam. As Caliph, he continued to increase the size of the Empire and spread its fair and just laws.

Arab horses are some of the fastest in the world.

Rashidun warriors would ride into battle on speedy horses, taking the Romans and Persians by surprise.

From the small beginnings of Islam in
Makkah and Madinah, the Prophet 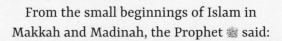 said:

"This matter (Islam) will certainly reach every place touched by the night and day..."
(Musnad Ahmad)

Madinah has fertile land and so many of the early Muslims were farmers.

The people of Madinah drank camel's milk, which made them strong.

Houses and masjids were built with mud bricks and thatched roofs.

Madinah is famous for its date fruits. Date-palm trees are found everywhere.

The Prophet  helped build the grand masjid in Madinah with his own hands.

Peaceful Palestine

Masjid al-Aqsa is in Jerusalem, where the Prophet ﷺ rose to the heavens after leading the other Prophets in prayer. Jerusalem was under Roman control, but Caliph Umar conquered it without any fighting.

Because Jerusalem was so important, the Church leader invited Caliph Umar, who was in Madinah, so he could personally hand him the keys to the city.

The people saw two Arab men on the horizon, one riding a donkey. Naturally, they assumed the one riding the animal was the Caliph.

Uthman bin Affan
(d. 656 CE)

Uthman was one of the first people to accept Islam. He married two of the Prophet's ﷺ daughters and was also a wealthy and generous businessman. When he became Caliph after Umar, he extended the Rashidun Empire into North Africa and India.

Ali bin Abi Talib
(d. 661 CE)

Ali was the cousin of the Prophet ﷺ and was married to his daughter Fatima. Ali was a brave warrior and a wise leader. After becoming Caliph, he moved the capital to Kufa in Iraq and spread Islam further east.

The Patriarch was gob-smacked when he found out that Umar took turns riding with his servant because the long and tiring journey. Umar was so humble that even when he made his grand entrance into Jerusalem, he let his servant take his rightful turn riding the donkey.

The Patriarch handed Umar the keys to Jerusalem, pleased that the city's new ruler would bring justice and prosperity. Jerusalem remained a peaceful place for hundreds of years under Muslim rule. Christians and Jews lived in harmony with the Muslims, who allowed them to practice their religions freely under their protection.

People-Power

The Ummah was growing so fast that the Rightly-Guided Caliphs had to build new cities and extend the Grand Masjids in Makkah and Madinah. They built road markers between each city to help people know how long was left on their journey. Whenever they took control of a new land, they worked with the people to make life fair and peaceful for everyone.

Many of the new citizens of the Rashidun Caliphate were not Muslim, but they were protected by the Muslim army in exchange for a small tax. This allowed them to enjoy security and freedom to

Bread, milk, dates and meat were common foods during the Rashidun rule.

practice their religion. However, the Rashidun Caliphs chose great governors who treated the people so well that many accepted Islam and became great leaders, scholars and soldiers.

Shifa bint Abdullah
(d. 640 CE)

Shifa was one of the few Companions of Prophet Muhammad ﷺ who knew how to read and write. Her real name was Layla, but she was nicknamed Shifa (cure) because she was an expert in medicine. She was so intelligent and trustworthy that Caliph Umar made her the Chief Officer of the markets in Madinah.

During the Rashidun Caliphate, the Quran was compiled into a physical book and spread to every part of the empire.

FOLLOW THE LEADER

The Prophet ﷺ said:

"Follow my example and the example of the Rightly-Guided Caliphs after me."
(Musnad Ahmad)

Many future Muslim leaders tried to follow the Prophet's ﷺ example in their own way, but none more so than Abu Bakr, Umar, Uthman and Ali. That's what made them 'Rightly-Guided.'

Even though the four Rashidun Caliphs faced different challenges, they always looked to the teachings of the Prophet ﷺ as the best example to follow in every part of their lives. This is how they became successful.

Let's be Amazing Muslims too

To be great leaders, we must first be great followers. And there's no better example to follow than the Prophet Muhammad ﷺ. The more of his Sunnah we follow, the better leaders we'll be. Let's learn the lessons from his life so we can grow and improve our character.

The Ambitious Umayyads

Lasted for 89 years from 661 to 750 CE

Under the Umayyads, the Muslim Empire became the largest superpower on the planet, stretching from Spain in the West all the way to India in the East.

The Umayyads were very skilled in managing their enormous empire. They built new cities, established a mint to make their own coins, and made Arabic the official language for all subjects. Under this thriving empire, many men and women became great scholars, memorising, studying and teaching the Quran and hadiths of the Prophet ﷺ and passing them down so we still read them today.

A Shining Example

Umar bin Abdul-Aziz was one of the well-known Umayyad Caliphs. As a young prince, he was blessed with a life of luxury. But Umar was also a keen student of the Islamic Sciences and the more he learnt, the more he appreciated the value of his faith.

When Umar became the Caliph, he used his power and wealth for good. He ordered that all the hadiths of Prophet Muhammad ﷺ be written down so that future generations would never lose them.

The empire collected so much Zakat that they could not find enough poor people to give charity to. Umar spent the wealth on building roads, canals and masjids for the people. Because of his fair rule, people prospered and there was a lot of barakah in the land.

Umar bin Abdil Aziz was the great grandson of Umar bin al-Khattab. That's why people call him 'The Second Umar'.

Atikah bint Yazid
(d. 743 CE)

Atikah was a member of the ruling family of the Umayyad empire and the wife of the Caliph Abdul-Malik bin Marwan. She was an expert in Islamic law and one of Abdul-Malik's most trusted advisors. She was especially charitable and always helped the needy.

Umayyad desserts were sweetened with fruits like figs, dates and apricots.

Where's the pattern on this rug from?

It's from Sindh in Northern India. Commander Muhammad bin Qasim just conquered that land.

The Umayyad's Grand Masjid in Syria

To establish their great empire, the Umayyads minted coins with Arabic letters and included 'La-ilaha-illallah, Muhammad-Rasul-Allah' for all to read.

During the reign of Caliph Walid I, the growing Muslim community in Syria needed a place to pray, so a grand masjid was built on an ancient site in Damascus. More than 12,000 people from areas as far as Egypt, Persia, India, Greece and Morocco helped to build it. It took almost nine years to complete and cost more than 60,000 gold dinar coins. At the time, it was one of the largest masjids in the world, and remains as a symbol of Muslim triumph today.

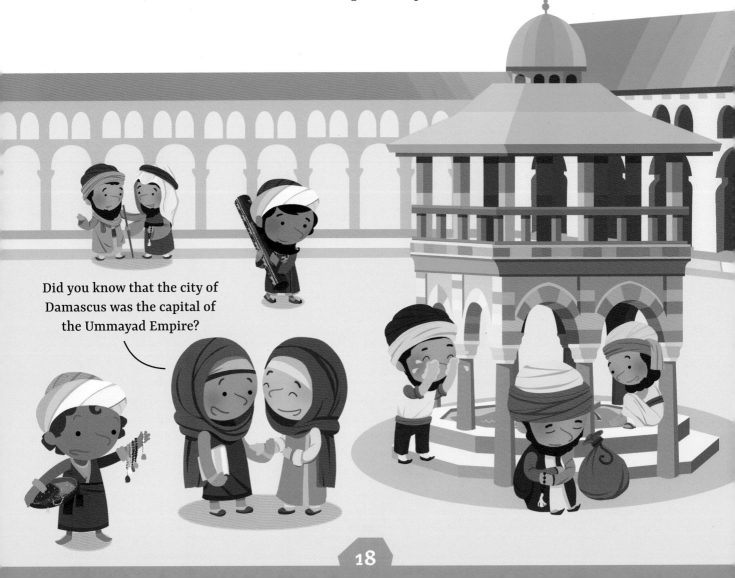

Did you know that the city of Damascus was the capital of the Ummayad Empire?

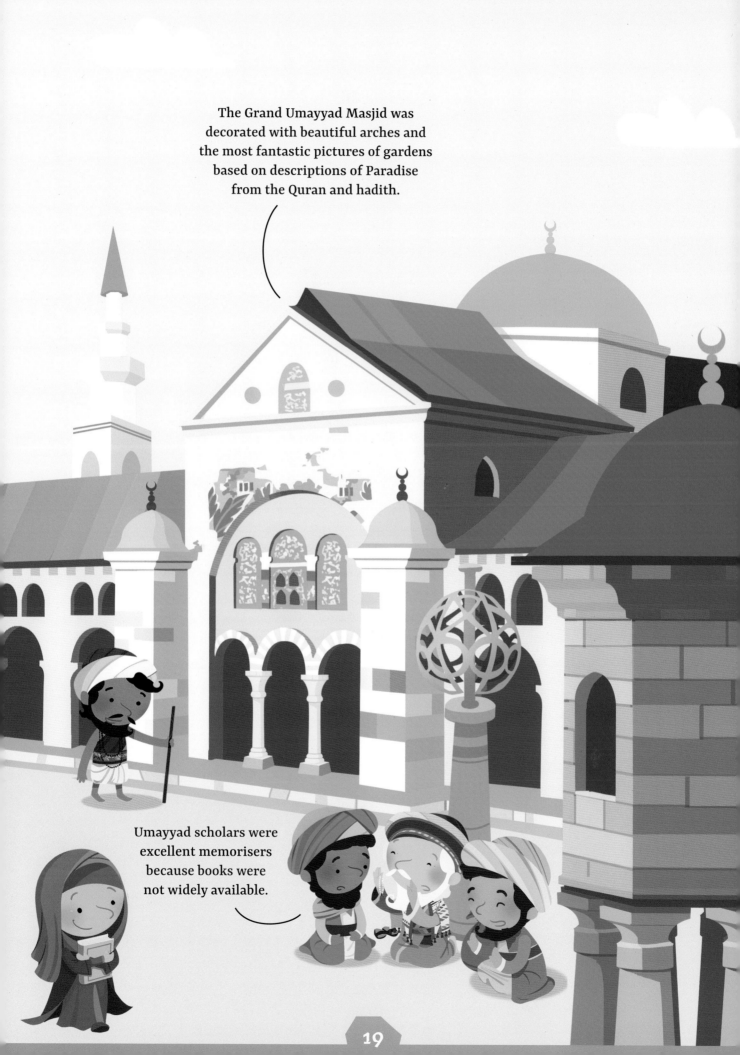

The Grand Umayyad Masjid was decorated with beautiful arches and the most fantastic pictures of gardens based on descriptions of Paradise from the Quran and hadith.

Umayyad scholars were excellent memorisers because books were not widely available.

Ibn Shihab Al-Zuhri
(d. 742 CE)

Al-Zuhri was a famous scholar raised in Madinah during the Umayyad era. Caliph Umar II asked him to write down collections of hadith, which were shared with schools and libraries across the Muslim world.

Building an Ummah

The citizens of the Umayyad Empire came from different lands, each following their own religion. Many accepted Islam, while others joined the Umayyad army and workforce because they enjoyed working alongside Muslims for the greater good.

During the Umayyad era, the famous Silk Road, which connected faraway lands and peoples, became a safe and prosperous route for trading foods, spices, pottery, and other goods. It was also important for the exchange of ideas.

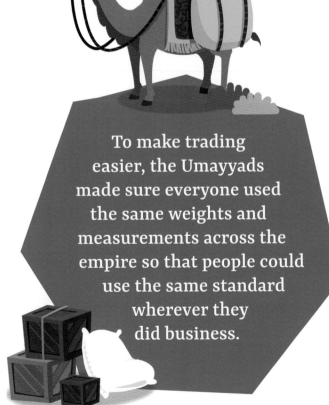

To make trading easier, the Umayyads made sure everyone used the same weights and measurements across the empire so that people could use the same standard wherever they did business.

ISLAM IS FOR EVERYONE

Allah says in the Quran:

"O Mankind! We created you from a single man and woman and made you nations and tribes so that you may know one another." (49:13)

The Umayyad Caliphs understood that no matter how different people are, we are all sons and daughters of Prophet Adam and Hawa.

As the Umayyads expanded their empire into new lands, they came across people of different races, languages and cultures. The rulers honoured these peoples by treating them fairly, just as Islam orders us to be just and understanding.

When people saw how respectful Muslims were about their differences, they couldn't help but embrace Islam. In turn, they made the Muslim community more diverse.

Let's be Amazing Muslims too

We can always learn something from a new culture, country, and language. Even if we're not all alike, there's usually something helpful we can understand from others. The Prophet ﷺ said, 'Wisdom is the lost property of a Believer. Wherever he finds it, he is most worthy of it.' (Tirmidhi)

The Awesome Andalusians

Lasted 781 years from 711 to 1492 CE

After the Umayyads conquered Spain, they established one of the greatest centres of knowledge and trade. Muslims, Christians and Jews lived with one-another in peace and prosperity.

When the Umayyads lost their power in the Middle East, they held on to the land of al-Andalus in modern-day Spain. Muslims continued to rule over al-Andalus for nearly 800 years. During that time, they built a vibrant society that welcomed people from other cultures. Arabic was made the first language, and an advanced community blossomed with beautiful schools, ideas and new inventions.

FRANCE

ITALY

ANDALUSIA

Cool Cordoba

The Andalusian city of Cordoba was a shining light in Europe. It was home to a great university where Muslims, Jews and Christians all studied together and advanced in the sciences. Cordoba had 50 hospitals, hundreds of years before other big cities like Paris and Berlin.

Cordoba was such a famous city that nobles and wealthy landowners in European cities sent their families to study in the safety of the Andalusian Empire. Cordoba became famous for its luxurious palaces, gardens, masjids, and waterways. The countryside was full of farms where abundant fruits and vegetables were harvested. If you were looking for quality foods, leather, pottery, weapons or silk, Andalusia was the place to shop.

Khalaf al-Zahrawi
(d. 1013 CE)

Al-Zahrawi grew up in Cordoba, the capital of the Andalusian Empire, during its golden age. He was a medical expert and wrote a book on medicine in a whopping 30 volumes. He also invented over 200 surgical tools and was nicknamed the 'Father of Surgery'.

In Cordoba alone, there were more than 700 masjids and 300 public baths. Since purity is half of iman, Spanish Muslims strove to keep their hearts and bodies clean.

When I grow up, I want to be a scientist.

In-sha-Allah!

A Sight to Behold

One of the finest buildings constructed in the Andalusian Empire, was the Alhambra Palace and fortress in the grand city of Granada. It took almost 20 years to build and it still stands today.

Alhambra rests on a mountain, overlooking Granada and the countryside. The palace was designed by skilled architects who added detailed arches, pillars, roofs and tiled walls full of colour.

The Sultans held special gatherings at Alhambra, inviting delegations from other parts of Europe and the Middle East. Even today, visitors marvel at its intricate calligraphy, peaceful gardens and soothing water fountains.

We can still visit the Alhambra Palace today and see how the talented Andalusians lived.

Soldiers in the Andalusian army came from Spain and North Africa.

Super Sevil-ians

Seville was one of the great cities of the Andalusian Empire. It was a centre of international trade thanks to its unique water flow system which farmers used to grow all kinds of fruits like cherries, pomegranates and figs. The Muslims even introduced orange trees to Seville, giving the streets a bright splash of colour.

It was a relaxing city, full of wonderful houses of worship, gates, courtyards and bath houses.

Queen Sabihah
(d. 999 CE)

Sabihah was the wife of Caliph al-Hakam II. She was incredibly smart and helped run the Andalusian state alongside her husband and sons. People loved her because she kept taxes low.

Seville was so grand that it became known as the 'Pearl of Andalusia'

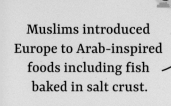

Muslims introduced Europe to Arab-inspired foods including fish baked in salt crust.

The Start of Something Global

While most of Europe was suffering in the Dark Ages, Andalusia was a prosperous wonderland full of bright people and new ideas. Islamic scholars wrote explanations of the Quran and hadith, and works on Islamic law, history and poetry.

Science was very important to the Andalusians. They not only wrote detailed books on medicine, chemistry and physics, but they also discovered all kinds of new inventions like the triangular-shaped sail which helped ships steer the seas, no matter which way the wind blew. They also excelled in geography, drawing better maps to help travellers.

Astrolabes helped scholars measure the position of the sun and other stars.

Abbas ibn Firnas
(d. 887 CE)

Ibn Firnas was a polymath. That means he was an expert in lots of sciences and arts. At the age of 60, he invented the first ever glider plane made of silk, wood and bird feathers. His invention made him the first human in history to fly.

Some Andalusian scholars were fascinated by the stars. They improved tools like the astrolabe to chart different constellations in space. This knowledge helped them map the world and design calendars to keep count of the special months and days in Islam.

Many of the great works written during this period were later translated into Latin so Andalusian knowledge spread throughout Europe and the rest of the world.

STRIVE FOR EXCELLENCE

The Prophet Muhammad ﷺ said:

"Allah has written everything to be done with excellence."
(Sahih Muslim)

The Muslims of Andalusia followed this hadith in every field. They did their very best to build beautiful cities with lovely palaces, masjids, gardens, hospitals and schools.

In the same way, they showed excellence in researching Islamic knowledge, writing many classical books. The explanation of the Quran by al-Qurtubi, for example, is still available today in over 20 volumes.

Andalusian scholars equally excelled in the sciences and technology, inventing new devices and improving old ones that helped everyone, not just the Muslims.

Let's be Amazing Muslims too

We can apply excellence in the things we do every day. When we write, we can write in our best handwriting. When we speak, we can use the best of words. When we listen, we can pay good attention. And when we worship Allah, we can do it with all our heart.

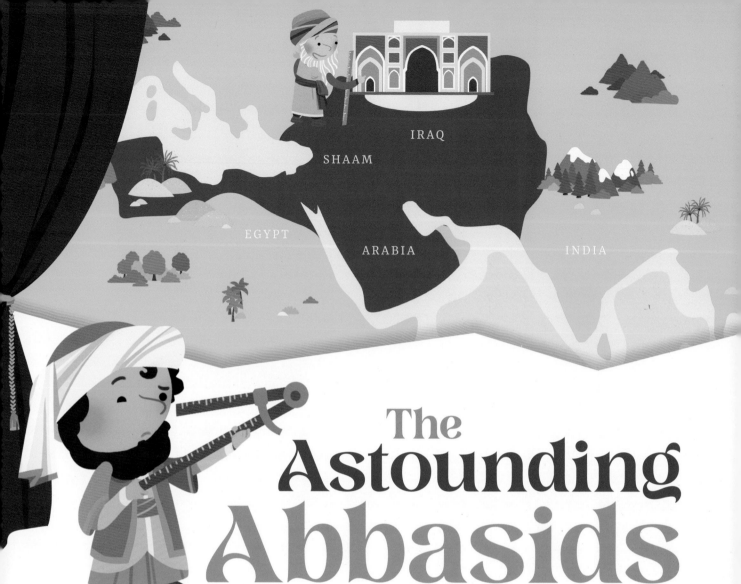

The Astounding Abbasids

Lasted 767 years from 750 to 1517 CE

From their capital in Baghdad, the Abbasids extended the Muslim world. They advanced science by translating works from other civilisations and then researching their own ideas.

The Abbasids took Islamic civilisation to greater heights, attracting more people to Islam. Non-Muslim admirers called this era the Golden Age of Islam. The Abbasids extended the borders of the Muslim empire, reaching as far as Indonesia. Wherever they ruled, they built centres of knowledge and new facilities for people, including the world's first public hospital.

My name is Abul Hasan ibn Ishaq and I'm inventing the world's first telescope.

More than one million people lived in Baghdad. At its peak, it was the biggest city on earth and was filled with dazzling masjids, gardens, zoos, and souks.

Brilliant Baghdad

Papyrus to Paper

The Abbasids learned the art of making paper from the Chinese, which had been a well-kept secret for many years. Soon after, factories across the Abbasid Empire began mass-producing paper. As a result, more people learned to read and write.

Paper changed the flow of knowledge. Now it was much easier to write and send information from one place to another.

The Abbasids moved the capital of their empire to Iraq by building a new city called Baghdad. It took 100,000 workers more than five years to make. Baghdad was a bustling city designed in a circular shape, with the Caliph's palace in the centre, surrounded by houses, masjids, markets, and schools. This made it easy for everyone to access the city centre, where many of the main events took place.

The palace in Baghdad even had a special piece of land next to it, full of exotic animals that the Abbasid rulers would hunt and eat.

Baghdad became known as 'Madinat as-Salam' (The City of Peace). And because it was located on a trade route and beside two rivers, the city became very wealthy.

A Fascinating House of Discovery

The Abbasids loved learning. In Baghdad, they built a school called the House of Wisdom or Bait al-Hikmah, which became a centre for all types of knowledge. It contained a massive library of manuscripts, research rooms and an observatory.

Zubaidah bint Ja'far
(d. 831 CE)

Zubaidah was a noble Abbasid princess who later married the famous Caliph Harun al-Rashid. She loved the Quran so much that her palace would be filled with women reciting it every day.

She also cared for people a great deal and ordered water reservoirs to be built for pilgrims in Makkah.

The scholars who visited there were recognised around the world as leaders in mathematics, the arts, and medicine.

As a result, they invented and discovered all sorts of things like astrolabes for navigation and algebra to solve maths problems.

This meeting ground for brilliant minds was also a hub for one of the greatest translation movements ever. Scholars translated ancient works in Greek and Persian into Arabic. The Abbasids took the best of ancient works and improved them with their own contributions.

The Abbasids' love for learning was inspired by the Quran's teachings to think and explore.

The House of Wisdom is open to both men and women.

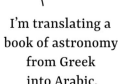

I'm translating a book of astronomy from Greek into Arabic.

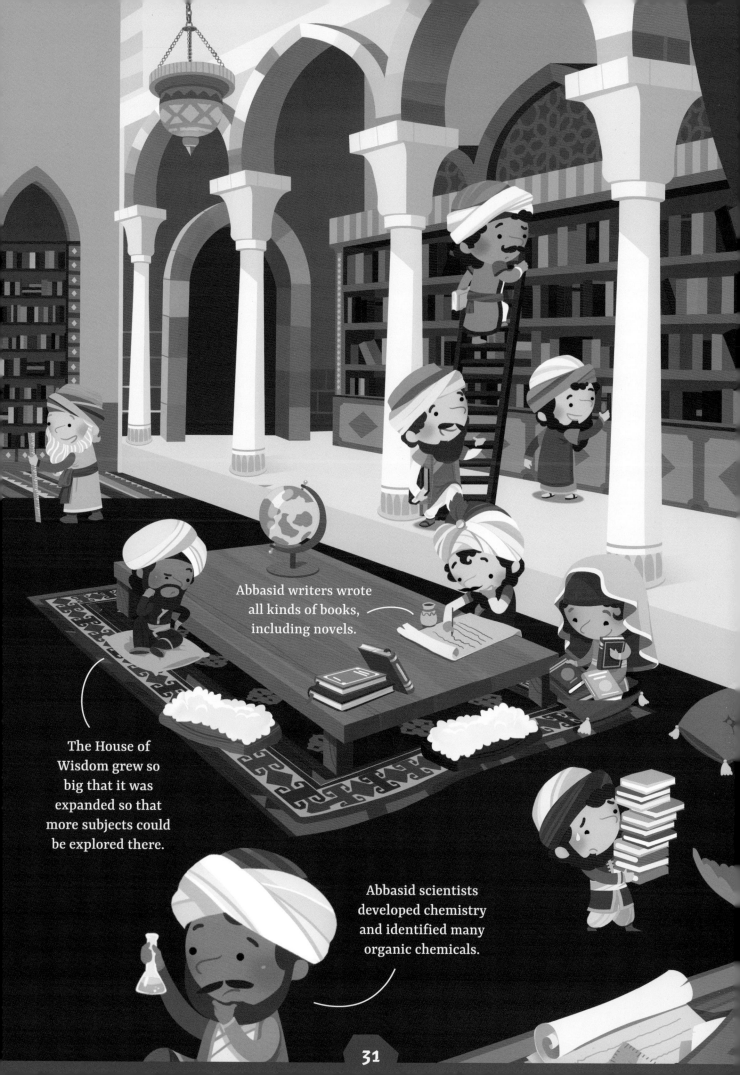

Abbasid writers wrote all kinds of books, including novels.

The House of Wisdom grew so big that it was expanded so that more subjects could be explored there.

Abbasid scientists developed chemistry and identified many organic chemicals.

Muhammad al-Khwarizmi
(d. 847 CE)

Al-Khwarizmi was a genius Muslim scholar, mathematician, astronomer and geographer. He introduced the principles of algebra and algorithms, which are still used today in smartphones, the internet and AI.

Al-Khwarizmi invented algebra to help understand inheritance in the Quran.

Everybody's Welcome

Seated in their capital, the Abbasid rulers were excellent diplomats who communicated with kings in far away lands. Once, the Caliph Harun al-Rashid sent Charlemagne, the King of the Franks in France, gifts including an elephant and a clock run by water.

Good relations encouraged trade, sharing knowledge and peaceful interactions. This allowed Abbasid subjects to live in harmony and help earn the empire respect and admiration from their neighbours.

With so many Arabs and non-Arabs living side-by-side, the empire flourished because it encouraged unity and working together. Judges, inventors, doctors and teachers worked together to make living standards better and this allowed the Abbasids to grow the Muslim empire's reputation around the world.

SEEKING KNOWLEDGE

The Prophet Muhammad ﷺ said:

> "Whoever takes a path in order to seek knowledge, Allah will make the path to Paradise easy for him."

(Abu Dawud)

From this hadith, the Abbasids understood the importance of knowledge. Their rulers made paper widely available and built places of learning that were free for all to experience.

As a result, the Abbasid Empire produced countless scholars, including those who wrote the famous six books of hadith which we still read and study today: Bukhari, Muslim, Abu Dawud, Tirmidhi, Nasa'i and Ibn Majah.

Other scholars pursued knowledge about the world and made new inventions and important discoveries that have helped future generations.

Let's be Amazing Muslims too

Allah has blessed us with a mind to think and grow. Just as the Abbasid scholars masterfully blended the teachings of Islam with languages, mathematics, and science, we too have the power to make a discovery or design a masterpiece in order to please Allah.

It all starts with a single spark of curiosity with faith. Let's embrace ours, and we might just change the world for the better while earning Jannah too.

ANATOLIA

SHAAM

AL-MAGHRIB

EGYPT

CENTRAL ASIA

KHORASAN

ARABIA

INDIA

The Sensational Seljuks

Lasted 157 years
from 1037 to 1194 CE

The Seljuk State was built by brave Turkic people from Central Asia who accepted Islam and moved through Iraq to the lands of Anatolia. They were faithful warriors and shielded Muslim lands from attack.

The Seljuks built caravanserais as resting places for travellers.

The Walking Library

A hadith tells us that every one-hundred years, Allah sends a person who will revive the religion of Islam. During the Seljuk era, this special person may well have been Imam al-Ghazali.

Al-Ghazali was born in Persia and became a talented scholar of the Islamic sciences. At the age of 33, he was the head teacher of the famous Nizamiyyah University in Baghdad, one of the finest places of learning in the world at the time. He wrote dozens of classical books that are still studied today.

During one of his journeys, a thief cornered Al-Ghazali. The Imam offered all of his belongings except

Seljuk artists were highly skilled. Arabic Calligraphers could write phrases in different styles, including animal shapes.

Seljuk artists were inspired by Allah's creation.

his precious books. The thief asked, what's the point of this knowledge if it could so easily be taken away? So, Al-Ghazali spent the rest of his life memorising everything he had learned, which is why he was called the 'walking library'.

The Selfless Seljuks

The emirs of the Seljuk State knew that their forefathers came from humble beginnings. That's why when they came into power, they made sure everyone had the opportunity to learn and grow. They built many new madrasahs and schools so that their people would receive a good education, often for free.

Persian Power

The Seljuks were not originally Arabs and so they spoke the Persian language. After coming into power, they ensured that Persian, alongside Arabic, was taught throughout the empire. The result was a rich, colourful and creative culture driven by Persian artists, poets and scholars. They showed us how people can adapt to Islam no matter which culture they are from.

Nur al-Deen Zengi
(d. 1174 CE)

Nur al-Deen was a brilliant Seljuk General and Emir of Syria. With the help of Allah, he was able to defeat the Crusaders and stop them from capturing Syria and harming innocent people.

Seljuk cuisine includes many different types of soup.

TAKING INITIATIVE

The Seljuks lived during a particularly difficult time when the Crusaders were harming innocent people. But the Seljuks remembered the words of the Prophet Muhammad ﷺ who said:

"Whoever among you sees evil, let him change it with his hand. If he cannot, then with his words. If he cannot, then with his heart and this is the least of faith."

(Sahih Muslim)

The Seljuks had the power to stop evil so they fought the Crusaders and protected the people. Even though the Seljuks became so powerful that they could have started their own empire, they still respected the Abbasids and let them remain in power. In doing so, they created a united front, much to the annoyance of the Crusaders.

Let's be Amazing Muslims too

Sometimes we see bad things happen around us, like someone getting bullied at school. But like the Seljuks, we don't bully and we don't allow others to bully us. Whether through our actions or our words, we have the power to make a difference. At the very least, let's never be pleased by evil and always stay on the side of the truth, even if it's against us.

We Seljuks were famous for our rugs. I'm having a break before I continue making another one.

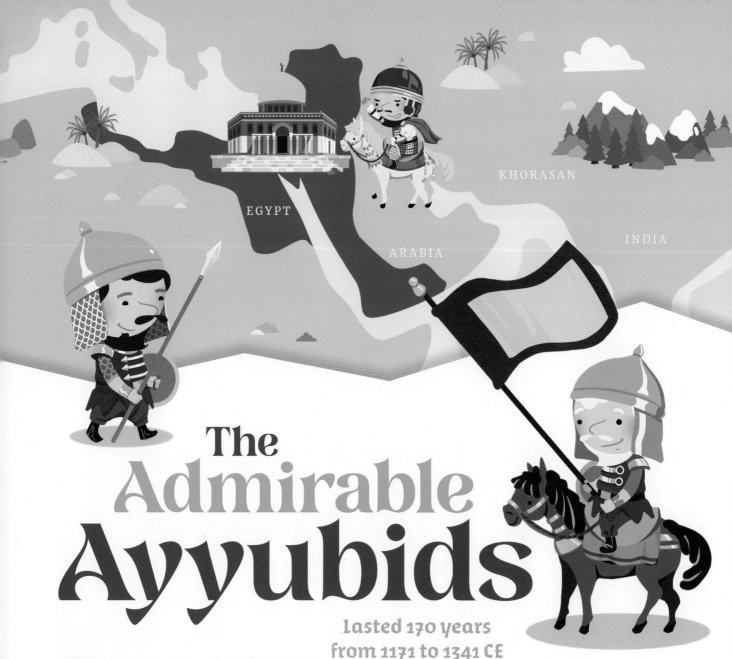

EGYPT

ARABIA

KHORASAN

INDIA

The Admirable Ayyubids

Lasted 170 years from 1171 to 1341 CE

The Ayyubids united the Muslim world and re-captured Jerusalem by defeating the Crusaders. They also spread knowledge throughout Egypt and Syria by opening lots of madrasahs.

When the Crusaders attacked Muslim lands and took Jerusalem, much of the Muslim world fell into despair. Alhamdulillah, during this difficult time, the Ayyubid Emirs emerged as heroes. From their base in Egypt, the new empire spread into Syria, Yemen and Iraq and built schools, hospitals and forts.

The Taste of Freedom

462 years after Caliph Umar bin Al-Khattab from the Rashidun Caliphate conquered Jerusalem, thousands of Crusaders from Europe invaded the city, killing many of the citizens of this sacred place.

Almost 100 years after the Crusaders' capture of Jerusalem, Sultan Salah al-Deen, now leader of Egypt, united small Muslim towns into one strong force. Salah al-Deen's army defeated a

Salah al-Deen
(d. 1193 CE)

Salah al-Deen was born in Iraq in a Kurdish family. As a child, he set his sights on freeing Jerusalem. He worked with Seljuk leader, Nur al-Deen Zengi to defend Egypt. Years later, he united the Muslims and achieved his childhood goal of liberating Masjid al-Aqsa.

huge Crusader army at the famous Battle of Hattin in 1187 CE and, soon after, marched into Jerusalem to restore peace.

Salah al-Deen followed the example of the Prophet Muhammad ﷺ by not taking revenge. He allowed Muslims, Jews and Christians to live together in peaceful Jerusalem once again.

Around 40,000 Muslim soldiers fought in the Battle of Hattin.

Salah al-Deen's Mimbar

When Salah al-Deen was a young boy, he heard about a carpenter who built a beautiful mimbar. Many people wanted the mimbar for their local masjid, but the carpenter refused. He said that it was designed only for Masjid al-Aqsa. The people told him that Jerusalem was under Crusader control, to which the carpenter replied, "Then let a brave soul rise to free Jerusalem." This story inspired Salah al-Deen, and several years later when he conquered the city, he placed the mimbar in Masjid al-Aqsa.

The last Ayyubid ruler was Shagarat al-Durr, and she was the first woman to rule Egypt since the time of Cleopatra.

The Ayyubids educated people on Islam by supporting schools, including the famous al-Azhar University in Cairo, which remains a major centre for learning Islam today.

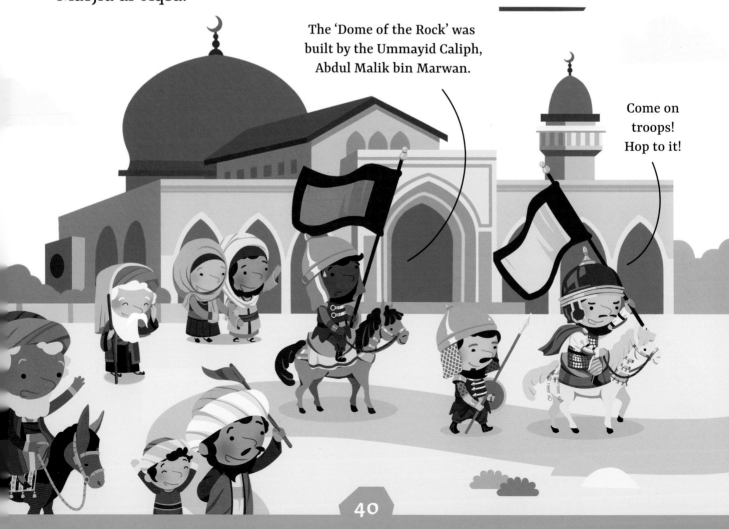

The 'Dome of the Rock' was built by the Ummayid Caliph, Abdul Malik bin Marwan.

Come on troops! Hop to it!

NEVER GIVE UP

The Ayyubids could not rest knowing that the Crusaders occupied the holy city of Jerusalem. What makes matters worse is that the Crusaders harmed so many Muslims, Jews and even other Christians. The Ayyubids found strength in the following verse of the Quran in which Allah describes good Muslims as those:

"who, when they are attacked, defend themselves." (42:39)

The Ayyubids gathered their forces and marched to Jerusalem, knowing that the battle would be fierce. But they were not afraid because Allah tells us in the Quran:

"Do not lose heart, and do not lose hope, for you will overcome them if you are true believers." (3:139)

And just as Allah promised, the Ayyubids stayed true to their faith and defeated the Crusaders. But unlike their enemy, the Ayyubids were fair and did not seek revenge. They allowed the Crusaders to stay or leave Jerusalem in peace.

Let's be Amazing Muslims too

Just like Salah al-Deen, let's remember that even in the face of hardships, the mercy of Allah can transform challenges into triumphs. Allah is able to do all things. It's us who have to stay strong in our faith, pour our hearts into our work, and be patient. With iman and courage, we will succeed and move forward in life, in-sha-Allah!

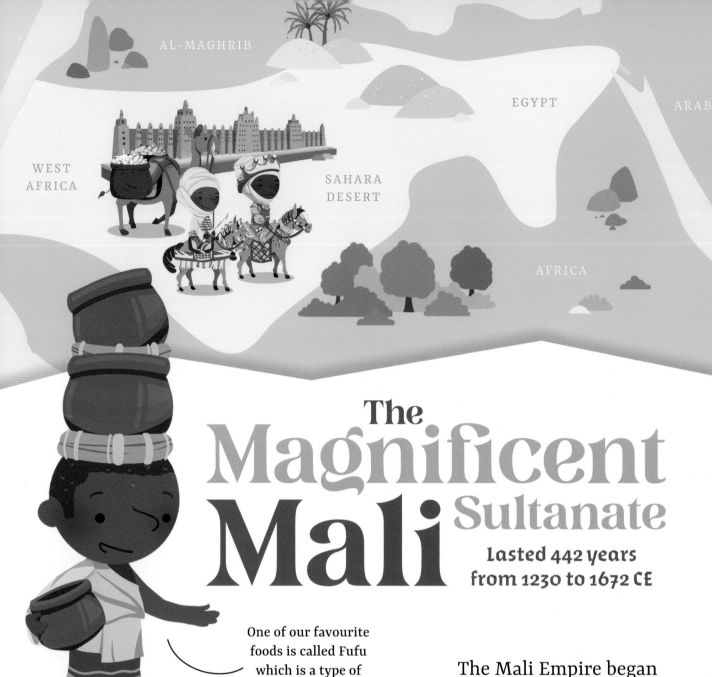

AL-MAGHRIB

EGYPT

ARABIA

WEST
AFRICA

SAHARA
DESERT

AFRICA

The Magnificent Mali Sultanate

Lasted 442 years from 1230 to 1672 CE

One of our favourite foods is called Fufu which is a type of Yam. It's Yammy!

The Mali Sultanate was one of the greatest empires in Africa. Its rulers controlled heaps of precious metals and minerals which they traded with their neighbours, and as far as Europe and the Middle East.

The Mali Empire began when the Kangaba people decided they did not like their mean ruler. They quickly established a kingdom based on justice and soon controlled West Africa. They became wealthy by harvesting salt and mining gold. They spent their wealth establishing schools, roads and masjids across the land.

Mansa Musa
(d. 1337 CE)

Mansa Musa was the most famous ruler of the Mali Sultanate. During his reign, the empire grew enormously rich and he became the richest man in history. He spent a lot of his wealth on good causes.

Mali to Makkah

In the year 1324 CE, Mansa Musa decided to perform Hajj, one of the five pillars of Islam. Being the wealthiest man on the planet, he wanted his people to come along too. So he arranged an all-expenses-paid trip for 60,000 people and had 80 camels carrying gold for the journey.

On their travels, Mansa Musa and his people visited many important cities, including Cairo, which was ruled by the Mamluks. The king spent large amounts of gold building wells and masjids along the way. In fact, he spent so much in charity that he had to borrow money on the return journey. To add to that, the amount of gold he spent in Egypt caused the prices of goods to rise for over 10 years.

Mansa means 'King', by the way.

Mum, I'm off to Hajj with Mansa Musa.

Make lots of dua when travelling.

Terrific Timbuktu

The centre of the Mali Empire was in the great city of Timbuktu. It was a popular place for trade and home to the Sankore Masjid, one of the most beautiful places of prayer on the planet. It was designed by a Muslim architect from Andalusia and was built with just wood and mud. Every year, after the rains, its walls are repaired with fresh mud, and it is still standing today.

At its peak, more than 100,000 people lived in Timbuktu of whom one quarter were scholars trained in Makkah and Egypt. This made Africa a great centre of learning.

Sankore University in the great city of Timbuktu was one of the world's greatest schools of knowledge. People in Mali today are still finding manuscripts that were once studied there.

The Mali Empire proved that having lots of wealth can be a great blessing because it helps start and grow good causes and trade.

The Mali Empire was so large that it took four months to travel from one end to the other by camel.

Just finished my book. Off to the library for another one.

44

MONEY WELL SPENT

Money tends to magnify what's in one's heart. So the cleaner our hearts, the more our money will help us. The Muslims of Mali remembered that the Prophet ﷺ said:

"Good wealth is excellent for a good person."

(Bukhari, Adab al-Mufrad)

As well as helping themselves, the Muslims of Mali spent large amounts of money looking after orphans and the poor and building wells and roads.

They understood that wealth is a blessing from Allah and can help us earn more good deeds for the hereafter. So they ensured they used their wealth to multiply their good deeds, knowing that Allah would reward them with more in this world and the next.

Let's be Amazing Muslims too

Everything we enjoy in life, like our homes, food and travel, is paid for by the wealth Allah has given us. Allah wants us to earn our wealth in a halal way and spend it in a halal way. And there's nothing wrong with having more wealth so long as we use it to please Allah. So, how do you plan to earn and spend your money?

The Marvelous Mamluks

Lasted 267 years from 1250 to 1517 CE

The Mamluks rose to power in Egypt and later spread into places like Syria and even India. They not only kicked the Crusaders out of Sham for good but also stopped the menacing Mongols from entering Africa.

Mamluk soldiers were Turkic slave-soldiers who fought for the Abbasids, Seljuks and Ayyubids until they became so powerful that they established their own empire. Cairo was their base and they quickly made Egypt and other lands centres of knowledge and trade between the East and West.

The Mamluks supported teachers and students from different schools of thought.

AL-MAGHRIB

SHAAM

EGYPT

ARABIA

SAHARA DESERT

Mamluks Meet the Mongols

The Mongols were a fierce army that trampled over most of the Muslim lands, including Baghdad. They then turned their sights on Egypt and met the Mamluks in Palestine at a place called Ain-Jalut, the same site where Prophet Dawud beat the mighty Jalut.

The Mamluks were smart and tricked the Mongols into thinking they were only few in number. But really, most of the Mamluk soldiers were hiding behind trees. They charged out of the forest and defeated the confused Mongol army. The entire Muslim world celebrated the victory.

Ibn Taymiyyah
(d. 1328 CE)

Ibn Taymiyyah was a genius Mamluk scholar who became an expert in so many sciences that he is still known today as the 'Shaykh of Islam.' As well as defending the Muslim world with his sword, he wrote many books defending Islam from people who tried to attack the religion.

The Mamluks were not only defenders of Islam, they also supported scholars, designers, scientists and builders.

KHORASAN

INDIA

Master-peace

Under the Mamluks, Cairo became a peaceful and powerful capital. It attracted some of the world's best artists and architects who created a unique style known today as the 'Mamluk tradition'.

Calligraphers designed beautiful copies of the Quran by hand while other people carved inspiring verses onto stone or wood. Artists painted elaborate patterns on clay pottery. Architects designed buildings with mighty domes and minarets that housed masjids, fortresses and shops.

Mamluk copies of the Quran are some of the most beautiful. One Mamluk Sultan even asked his chief calligrapher to write an entire copy by hand using gold ink.

Cairo became a visual wonder and tourists and traders flocked to its streets to buy its special goods. The Mamluks used this wealth to strengthen the Muslim world's economy after it was weakened by the invading Mongols.

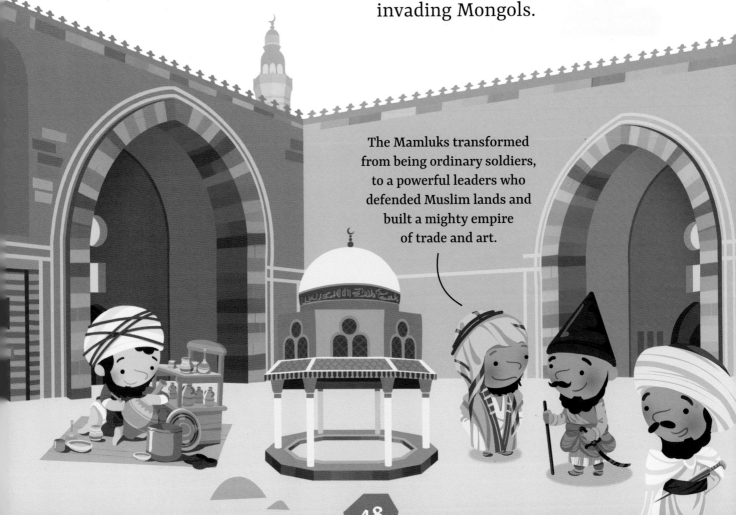

The Mamluks transformed from being ordinary soldiers, to a powerful leaders who defended Muslim lands and built a mighty empire of trade and art.

INNER BEAUTY

The Mamluks were no strangers to wonderful buildings and art. After all, they ruled Egypt, home to one of the greatest civilisations in history. But what made the Mamluks different was faith in Islam and the following hadith:

"Allah is Beautiful and He loves beauty."

(Tabarani, Mu'jam al-Awsat)

With this in mind, Mamluk rulers encouraged the best calligraphers, wood-carvers, builders, blacksmiths and artisans to make beautiful things. And so they did.

The result is that Cairo became famous for its unique art. Mamluk calligraphers developed their own style of Arabic calligraphy. It was so beautiful that many Mamluk copies of the Quran, buildings and everyday objects like plates feature Mamluk calligraphy.

Let's be Amazing Muslims too

We carry in our hearts the beautiful faith of Islam. Everything about this religion is beautiful, from our beliefs, our ways of worship, our values and traditions. And from this inner beauty comes the outer beauty of our work and actions, all celebrating Allah's blessings. Now let's ask ourselves, what beautiful work will we do in this world so we can enjoy a beautiful reward in the hereafter?

The Outstanding Ottomans

Lasted 623 years from 1299 to 1922 CE

The Ottomans ruled over a vast empire that spread Islam to Eastern Europe. People of many different cultures and religions lived peacefully under their rule for hundreds of years.

Turkic Muslim tribes in Asia established a powerful dynasty that quickly spread across parts of Europe and the Middle East. This empire was named after its founder, Osman, son of Ertuğrul, and the world came to know it as the 'Ottoman Empire'. It produced some of the most beautiful art, architecture, huge cannons and ships.

Merchants from all over the world visited Ottoman lands for high-quality goods and spices.

EASTERN EUROPE

CAUCASUS

EGYPT

ARABIA

INDIA

SAHARA DESERT

Bye-zantine

The Byzantine Empire was all that remained after the fall of the once-powerful Roman Empire. Its capital was Constantinople which was protected by gigantic walls and natural water defences. Under the leadership of Sultan Mehmed II, the Ottomans conquered the great city and renamed it Istanbul. But how did he manage to do this when so many rulers before him failed?

Over 100 Ottoman ships were sent to the battle but the Byzantines blocked their path with a large sea chain. Mehmed II came up with a clever idea: overnight, his men dragged their ships over a hill and bypassed the chain.

Sulayman the Magnificent
(d. 1566 CE)

Sulayman I was the longest-reigning Sultan of the Ottoman Empire. He ruled over 25 million people, and because of his expert leadership, the world knows him today as 'Sulayman the Great'.

Constantinople fell soon after and the long reign of the Romans came to an end. The Ottomans turned their new capital into a centre for trade, art and learning.

The early Ottoman Sultans had to master many subjects such as the Islamic Sciences, maths, languages, logic, archery and horse riding.

Istanbul is located on the Bosphorus Strait, which is great for fishermen like me.

Mehmed II was only 19 when he conquered Constantinople.

Mimar Sinan
(d. 1588 CE)

Sinan was a talented architect selected by Sultan Sulayman I as the Chief Architect of the Ottoman Empire. He built hundreds of beautiful palaces, masjids, museums, bridges and pools, many of which still stand today.

A hadith says that if I build a masjid, Allah will build a house for me in Jannah.

Squeaky Clean

The soaps we recognise today were first invented by the Abbasids, who mixed olive oil with scents. Soap continued to develop in the Muslim Worlds, and by the time the Ottomans arrived, they were used in hospitals, homes, and special bath-houses called 'hammams'.

Since purity and cleanliness are essential in Islam, Muslim towns enjoyed clean water supplies for wudu and baths. Ottoman hammams used soaps, oils and perfumes to turn the bathing ritual into a popular experience that spread to the rest of the world.

Salam and Salut!

The Ottomans ruled over so many people that their citizens spoke multiple languages, from Arabic to Romanian.

The Great Hagia Sophia

The Hagia Sophia was over a thousand years old before the Ottomans conquered Istanbul. It was known as one of the most famous cathedrals in the world, before Sultan Mehmed II turned it into a masjid. Tall minarets were added to the building, but the architects were keen to keep many original features of the building which can still be found today.

Ottoman artists and artisans were very creative. They added beautiful patterns to all kinds of things, including plates and pendants.

Ottoman soldiers were skilled archers and could shoot an arrow past 800 metres at a speed of over 200 km per hour.

Women Behind the Throne

Even though Ottoman Sultans were all men, their mothers and wives often helped to manage the affairs of the empire. These great women also gave good advice, spent on good causes and helped to build masjids under the order of the Sultans.

Arts and Crafts

The Ottomans loved the arts and encouraged their people to learn different crafts by building special schools and hiring the best teachers. Men and women would train for years in the art of miniature-painting, carpet-weaving, tile-making, pottery and embroidery.

The Ottomans were particularly fond of Arabic and Persian calligraphy. The famous Ottoman calligrapher Mustafa Izzet Efendi painted eight giant circles with the names of Allah, Muhammad ﷺ, Abu Bakr, Umar, Uthman, Ali, and the Prophet's grandsons Hasan and Husain. They were over seven meters wide, which meant that Mustafa had to paint them with a mop, rather than a paint brush.

Safiye Sultan
(d. 1619 CE)

Safiye was a great Ottoman leader and mother of Sultan Mehmed III. She helped her son govern the great empire. People would stop her carriage asking her for support knowing she would always try to help.

Wow! That's a lot of ink for one piece of calligraphy.

AIMING HIGH

The Prophet Muhammad ﷺ said:

"Allah loves the high aims and dislikes the lower ones."

(Tabarani, Mu'jam al-Awsat)

It's no surprise that the Ottomans always had big ambitions. They turned a small Turkic tribe living in the countryside into one of the strongest and largest empires that the world has ever seen.

Millions of people lived under Ottoman rule and the Sultans took their responsibility seriously. They knew that the Prophet ﷺ said:

"Each one of you is (like) a shepherd and is responsible for his flock. The leader is a guardian and is responsible for his people."

(Sahih Bukhari)

Taking care of things can be hard but Allah made it easy for the Sultans by giving them enough power, strength and intelligence. They used these qualities to create a united empire of different peoples, cultures and languages.

Let's be Amazing Muslims too

Let's always aim high because Allah can make anything happen. Whatever we want to be or do, whether it's a great leader, scholar, doctor, scientist or artist, let's remember to ask for Allah's help, work hard and be patient along the way. We can do it, in-sha-Allah!

The Charming Chinese Muslims

China was home to one of the world's leading Islamic centres of learning. Although Muslims never conquered China, they lived with non-Muslims under the Ming dynasty as one people. They even dressed the same and spoke the same language.

Lasted 276 years from 1368 to 1644 CE

After the fall of Mongol rule in China, a new and powerful dynasty was founded by Emperor Zhu Yuanzhang. He admired Islam and cared for the Muslims. Under his dynasty, a number of Muslims settled in China and some Chinese men and women accepted Islam. Many masjids and madrasahs were built in China during this time.

Zheng-He
(d. 1435 CE)

Zheng-He was a great Muslim politician, explorer and army general. He commanded gigantic ships and visited countries across Asia and Africa. He kept a diary and recorded all the exotic things he saw along the way, some of which he brought back to China.

Chinese Muslims developed their own recipes because the Quran tells us not to eat pork or drink wine.

Dragon Ships

Prince Zhu Di was one of the sons of Emperor Zhu. After his father's death, the Prince became Emperor and wanted to show the world how great the Ming dynasty was.

Every ship had eyes painted on the front.

Some of Zheng-He's ships were over 400 feet long and 170 feet wide. That's almost the size of a football pitch.

The Prince ordered his trustworthy Muslim advisor Zheng-He, to travel to other lands and sell Chinese products. Zheng-He took over 200 ships with him, some of which were gigantic, travelling like dragons across the seas.

He visited more than 30 countries and had many adventures. His army battled pirates and stopped over at different ports. During his travels, Zheng-He gave beautiful Chinese pottery to the people he met. He brought home some interesting plants and animals, including a giraffe.

A Warm Welcome

When the Mongols ruled Asia, many of the Muslims in that area lived and travelled in different parts of the continent, including China. After the Ming dynasty was founded, Emperor Zhu welcomed more Muslims to live, work and practise Islam peacefully under his rule. The Muslims were known for their excellent skills in making pottery, food and even Chinese-style masjids. Emperor Zhu was so impressed with the way that Muslims lived their lives that **he wrote a 100-line poem** praising their role model, the Messenger of Allah ﷺ.

Even though the Ming dynasty was not ruled by Muslims, its Muslim citizens followed the law. They got along with everyone without losing their faith.

Sa'd bin Abi Waqqas
(d. 674 CE)

During the Rashidun Caliphate, one of the Companions of the Prophet Muhammad ﷺ called Sa'd, is said to have visited China where he built the first masjid there. Sa'd was an expert archer and a great leader who also conquered Iraq.

"Mercy to the world, even to the ancients. His majestic path did away with all evil. His religion pure and true. Muhammad ﷺ, the noble and high one."

I wouldn't mind another cup of Chinese herbal tea.

CARE TO BE KIND

Kindness and mercy are two of the best qualities in human beings. The Prophet Muhammad ﷺ said:

"Allah is kind and He loves kindness."
(Sahih Muslim)

In another hadith, the Prophet ﷺ said:

"The merciful ones will be shown mercy by the Most Merciful (Allah)."
(Tirmidhi)

Kindness and mercy were just two of the qualities Muslims in China had. They showed these great qualities in how they did business, and lived with their non-Muslim neighbours. The result was that Chinese people of various languages, cultures and religions respected Muslims.

Let's be Amazing Muslims too

Sometimes, good manners open doors that can't be opened with force. When people meet us and see the beautiful manners of Islam we practice, they'll respect Muslims and our values. Plus, a kind person is much nicer to be around!

So much so that even the Emperor of the Ming Dynasty wrote a lovely poem about the Prophet ﷺ. Why? Because he knew that's who his Muslim subjects followed.

The Amazing Aceh Sultanate

Lasted 407 years from 1496 to 1903 CE

MALAYSIA

ACEH

The Aceh Sultanate was the first Muslim superpower in the Indonesian islands. Led by brave rulers and warriors, the islands were protected from Dutch and Portuguese colonisers.

Aceh was a centre of business, famous for its honest traders, spices, metals and elephants. It also became a popular place for Islamic knowledge. Scholars from all over Asia and the Middle East taught in its schools. Arabic texts on Islam were translated to the local Malay language.

Rice is one of the staple foods in the Indonesian islands. Even our desserts have rice in them.

Cut Nyak Dhien
(d. 1906 CE)

Cut Nyak Dhien lived as a learned housewife, until one day, her husband was killed by an invading Dutch army. Then she became a fearless warrior, fighting the Dutch. After many years, she won the ultimate prize of being a martyr for the sake of Allah.

Queen Elizabeth I once sent a letter to the Sultan of Aceh by ship. The ship was only allowed to pass into the Aceh Sultanate once Malahayati gave it permission.

You're an inspiration to us all!

Where are you sailing off to today Malahayati?

I'm just off to protect the sultanate from the Dutch. I'll be back in time for dinner.

Freedom-Fighters

The Aceh Sultanate was a wonderful place full of riches and good-hearted people. The Dutch and Portuguese had strong naval armies and wanted all of Aceh's resources. Alhamdulillah, Aceh's army gave them both a tough time and defended the Muslim lands for hundreds of years. The Dutch and Portuguese tried to bribe the Acehnese Muslims to divide them, but Aceh was not for sale.

One of the toughest Acehnese warriors was Malahayati, the daughter of a respected admiral. After studying Islam in one of Aceh's madrasahs, she followed in her father's footsteps and joined the Acehnese navy.

She was so talented that she soon became the first female admiral in history and defended the sultanate for many years.

The House of Allah

One of the finest masjids in all of Indonesia is Masjid Bait al-Rahman. The masjid was built by Sultan Nur al-Alam just before the Dutch began their most serious attacks on the Indonesian islands soon after. For 30 years, the Acehnese protected their beloved sultanate. The Dutch became so frustrated that they offered to rebuild Masjid Bait al-Rahman (which they had damaged) to convince the Acehnese to stop the war.

The Dutch did end up controlling Indonesia, but Alhamdulillah, the Muslims later fought them and freed their land. The Masjid still stands today, with three wonderful domes, reminding us of Aceh's brave history.

Ibn Battuta, the famous explorer, travelled to the Aceh Sultanate and recalled seeing over 300 war elephants in the Sultan's army.

The Aceh Sultanate was an amazing powerhouse of knowledge and trade. It never fully surrendered to colonising forces.

Colonisers are not welcome here.

A GREAT BUSINESS DEAL

The Prophet Muhammad ﷺ said:

"Allah Almighty will give a person Paradise because he was easy-going in buying and selling, and in paying debts and seeking repayments."

(Musnad Ahmad)

Hadiths like this encouraged Muslims to be easy-going in business. When Muslims traded with the people of Indonesia, the locals accepted Islam because they were so impressed with the good manners of the Muslims.

The Muslims of Indonesia, including those who lived in the Aceh Sultanate, continued this tradition of being honest in business, especially when dealing with debts. This not only made them wealthy, but also earned them respect from others.

Let's be Amazing Muslims too

When we show the best side of our character, we not only increase in our iman, but we also help others see the effect that our faith has on us. So let our good behaviour be something we can please Allah with.

KHORASAN

CHINA

INDIA

The Mighty Mughals

Lasted 331 years from 1526 to 1857 CE

T he Mughals were India's most powerful empire and had a well-trained army. They spread Islamic art, textiles, culture, and spices throughout the world.

Mughal land covered modern-day India, Pakistan and Bangladesh.

Muslims first conquered parts of North India during the Umayyad era under the command of a General called Muhammad bin Qasim. But it wasn't until several hundred years later, and many empires in between, that most of India came into the hands of the Mughals.

Riches of the East

The Mughal Empire was one of the most powerful and wealthy in history. Through its cultivation and trade of spices, cotton, rice and tea, the empire grew incredibly rich, and its emperors spent their wealth on decorated buildings, masjids, gardens, water reservoirs and bridges.

The Mughals also introduced special outdoor kitchens to feed the poor and a financial support system for less fortunate citizens who could not afford basic food and shelter. They even built free schools, and their scholars excelled in Islamic studies, medicine and poetry.

The capital of the Mughal Empire was Delhi, which was surrounded by towering walls with lavish gates. The city boasts one of India's largest masjids (nicknamed Jama Masjid). It was built almost entirely from beautiful red bricks.

Emperor Aurangzeb
(d. 1707 CE)

Aurangzeb was one of the mightiest Mughal rulers and he was dedicated to Islam. He expanded the empire to its largest extent and funded countless scholars, books and schools.

Jama Masjid has enough space for 20,000 people to pray all at once, and it still gets busy.

I could pray at home, but praying with my brothers and sisters in the masjid is 27 times more rewarding.

Shah Wali-Allah Dehlawi
(d. 1763 CE)

Wali Allah was one of the brightest Mughal scholars. He encouraged Indian Muslims to get along even if they had different opinions. He also wrote many books that are still studied around the Muslim world.

The Taj Mahal was decorated by nearly 20,000 artists.

The Taj Mahal is built with ivory marble.

The Crown of India

Emperor Aurangzeb's father was Shah Jahan. He was a warrior, statesman and fan of beautiful art, poetry and architecture. At age 20, he married Mumtaz Mahal, whom he loved dearly. Sadly, she passed away a few years after giving birth to Aurangzeb. Shah Jahan ordered his architects to build a beautiful palace in her honour. The Taj Mahal includes a masjid, a guest house, lush gardens and plenty of water fountains. Its walls are lined with verses from the Quran written in Arabic calligraphy.

Today, the Taj Mahal is one of the most visited places on earth, making it one of the seven wonders of the world.

Smart Muslims

The Mughals cared for Islamic scholars and used judges to help them keep law and order. They supported madrasahs with scholarships so that students could focus on their studies. This support also gave authors the time and freedom to research and write excellent works in Arabic and Persian.

The Taj Mahal took 22 years in total to build and is decorated with beautiful floral patterns and calligraphy.

Persian Poets

Like the Ottomans, the Mughals ruled a vast land of people who spoke different languages. They encouraged people to learn Persian because it was rich in words and meanings. That's why so many Muslim and Hindu Persian poets came from Mughal India.

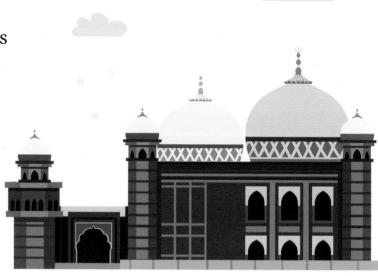

Positive Princess

Zeb-un-Nisa was a Mughal princess and daughter of Emperor Aurangzeb. She was incredibly bright and had memorised the whole Quran by age seven.

She had her own private library and skilled tutors who taught her the Arabic language, Persian poetry, calligraphy, as well as mathematics and astronomy.

Zeb-un-Nisa was also generous to the poor, widows and orphans. She often paid the expenses of Hajj pilgrims. Her father was so impressed by her character and knowledge that he often discussed matters of state with her and would heed her advice and counsel.

The Mughals turned South Asia into a wonderful place full of vibrant cities and amazing buildings. They spread Islam and encouraged Muslims to live alongside their Hindu and Buddhist neighbours in peace.

Emperor Aurangzeb was so happy when his daughter Zeb-un-Nisa memorised the Quran that he gifted her teacher 30,000 gold coins. Wow!

LOVE OF LEARNING

The Prophet Muhammad ﷺ said:

"Seeking knowledge is a duty for every Muslim."

(Ibn Majah)

We learned that education was very important to the Mughals as it was to all of the Amazing Muslim Worlds. Leaders and citizens built madrasahs and supported teachers and students in all fields of learning, especially the Islamic Sciences. That's because knowledge of our faith is essential to leading an upright life that's pleasing to Allah. It's also important in shaping how we approach other subjects in a way that serves Allah while improving people's lives.

Let's be Amazing Muslims too

The more we learn, the more we understand the world and the better tools we have to make great contributions. But learning doesn't just happen in classrooms and through books. In fact, learning never stops. Every experience in life teaches us something, and we can use it to grow and improve our minds and guide our actions.

Now it's your turn!

There's so much more for us to discover about Islamic history. Let's continue our learning journey. Here are some fun projects to explore the Amazing Muslim Worlds.

Discover Islam

The main source and inspiration for all the Muslim Worlds was the religion of Islam. **Write a short essay** on at least five beautiful values Islam promotes and their fantastic effects on people's lives. Reflect on your own experience with these values and how they make a difference to your life. Some of these values can be found in this book.

Learn the Lands

The Muslim Worlds covered vast areas of the Earth that we have not mentioned yet, such as Central Asia, Sub-Saharan Africa and the Caucuses. **Draw a world map** showing some of the big cities in these lands, such as Isfahan, Fez or Bukhara.

Inspiring People

Islamic history is full of great scholars, leaders, scientists, inventors, artists and more. We've discovered a few of them in this book, but there are many others. Pick ten famous figures from the Amazing Muslim Worlds and **design biography cards** with their names, dates and main achievements.

Sciences

Muslims were pioneers in many subjects, from flight, surgery, fabrics, algebra and even coffee. **Design a poster** showing at least ten inventions made by people from the Muslim Worlds. For each invention, show a picture, the inventor and date it was made.

Epic Empires

We've explored only a few great empires in Islamic history. There are many more dynasties and leaders who made outstanding contributions to the world. **List at least five other empires** from the Amazing Muslim Worlds not mentioned in this book.

Arts

Islamic art was displayed on masjids, palaces, hospitals, homes, and gardens. There were also great contributions in acoustics and carpentry. **Collect pictures** of at least ten patterns from the Amazing Muslim Worlds and compile them in a short book with the origin and description of each one.

Culture

With the mixing of different cultures, the people in the Amazing Muslim Worlds spoke many languages, cooked delicious dishes, and designed unique clothing and perfumes. **Find the recipe for a dish** from the Amazing Muslim Worlds, and make the dish with the help of an adult.